First Published 2013

ISBN — 978-0-9891677-5-8

MassMedia.mobi Press
107A North Payne Street
Alexandria, Virginia 22314
Website: www.massmedia.mobi

DISCLAIMER: This is a work of fiction, although real historic events are also touched upon, and several actual persons have been fictionalized for inclusion in the narrative. Names, characters, businesses, places, events and incidents are either the products of the author's imagination or used in a fictitious manner. Any resemblance to actual persons, living or dead, or actual events is purely coincidental, or intended to be construed as artistic license.

ACKNOWLEDGEMENTS: The author wishes to thank the photo archivists from the Hillwood Museum Research Collections & Archive, the Kiplinger Library of the Historical Society of Washington, D.C., the prints and photographs division of the Library of Congress, the Martin Luther King Library's Washingtoniana Room photo archives, and Bart Daugherty of Sundial Camper for their assistance.

Contents

Chapter 1 – Safety First

Cameron and his buds rode their bikes along the sidewalks and bike lanes of Del Ray, passing authentic Sears cottages and the Avenue's commercial district. For years the neighborhood had played second fiddle to neighboring Old Town, whose weekly farmers' market was the nation's oldest still in operation. George Washington had frequented the original market, at a time when it featured livestock in stalls. Old Town Alexandria, with gas lamps at the front of many of its majestic row houses, had clearly once been the better side of the tracks.

Speaking of tracks, Del Ray was originally a company town, built by the Richmond-Washington Railroad consortium to provide housing for employees of the Potomac Yards transit hub, at one time the mid-Atlantic's busiest rail yard. The blue collar train yard crews, engineers, and carpenters who maintained the freight and refrigerated cars all lived there, with management in homes on the hill in nearby Rosemont. Some Del Ray homes still have attic floorboards and basement closets with stenciled railroad lettering, the 'surplus' having found its way home with employees ages ago. By the 1990s, remnants of Potomac Yard still existed, but by then were just windswept fields instead of rail yards. The tall control tower was long gone, but the original entrance sign remained in place right up to the bitter end. "Safety First" was its never out-of-style message. For decades, workers passed under that sign as they arrived and departed on their daily rounds.

Nowadays the popularity of the neighborhoods—Old Town Alexandria and Del Ray—was flip-flopped. Del Ray storefronts were hip and sought after, at a premium, for ethnic restaurants and boutiques. The value of the cottages had ballooned. Old Town, meanwhile, seemed to have more and more of a rotation of empty stores. (Even if Colonial-era Old Town couldn't compete with its own upstart neighborhood in terms of trendiness, it still considered itself superior to Georgetown, Washington, D.C.'s first settlement across the river and a few miles to the north.)

The boys stopped together at a crosswalk. Cameron sighed. "I don't like being twelve," he said. "You're not old enough to get a job or get a driver's license. All we can do is ride bikes all summer." "Don't be in a hurry to grow up, dude. Enjoy your youth," said Jay over his shoulder, as he pedaled past and took the lead position. "Jay, you talk like an old man, like you're *fifty* or something," Cameron commented. Zach used a speed-bump to try and pop a wheelie and said, "Well, I'm personally happy to have the summer to ride bikes."

After a bit they came to the intersection where Cameron's dad's office was located on the second floor of an old bank branch. "Let's stop at the garage behind my dad's office, I wanna show you somethin'."

The boys leaned their bikes against the small garage and entered the side door into darkness. In years past, the garage had been a sort of storage hub for a chain local bank branches. It had housed boxes and boxes of fluorescent tubes, carpet tiles and heavy metal signage displays that read "OPEN" in green or "CLOSED" in red. After years of consolidation and cost cutting, it had been abandoned, and Cameron's dad leased it. He maintained it, in addition to the office lease, as a place to store vintage cars. It was only a two car garage, but with careful maneuvering, it held three, even if they were jammed in at odd angles. Garage space for old cars is a rare commodity in an urban area.

Something about the junk built up around the perimeter of the garage made Jay think, 'Off Limits,' and he said, "Cam, are we supposed to be in here? Would your dad be mad?" Cameron said, "It's O.K. if we're here. My dad would be cool with it." As their eyes adjusted, they could make out the bulbous lines of an old VW bus. Cameron flicked on his phone's flashlight, and the emerald green and white two-tone paint scheme in the light's glow made their eyes widen and brought on smiles. Zach said, "Wow... cool bus, dude."

"Is this thing a camper?" Jay asked. "Uh huh," Cameron confirmed, pleased at the response his surprise was receiving. "Yup. It's a bus. And it's a camper. But it's really a 'hippie van'."

The boys opened the front and side doors and clambered on in. Jay got behind the wheel. "Awesome." He wrapped his arms around the oversized steering wheel and turned it back and forth, pretending to drive and peering ahead, as if they were cruising down the road. "We're hippies, guys! Cruisin!" he said.

Jay's antics had a way of making Cameron nervous. "Be careful, don't break anything." Zach, ever inquisitive, asked, "What really is a hippie? Are they druggies?" "It's not about drugs. It was 'flower power,' 'free love' and 'peace,' man!" Jay assured him. At eleven, did Jay even know what 'free love' meant? It didn't matter, he knew it fit, and how to use it in a sentence.

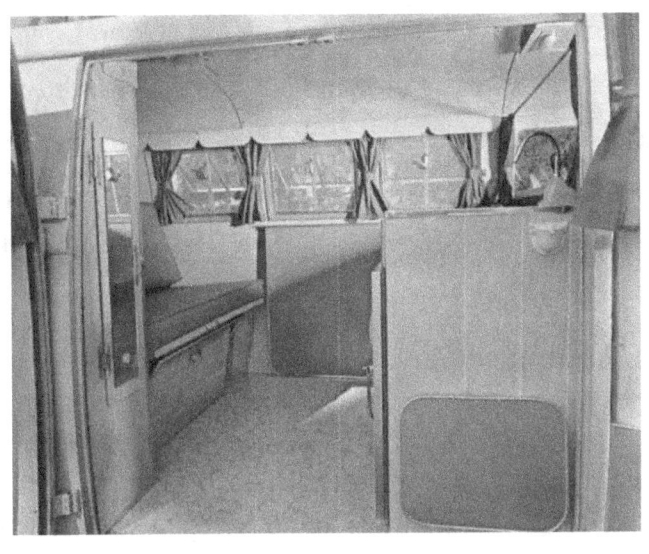

Cameron decided to bring them back on topic. "So you wanna hear the story? This bus was locked up in storage for over twenty years." The other two were astonished that anyone could own a vehicle this neat and not use it. "Why?" asked Jay. "It was parked on the third floor of a big ole warehouse in downtown D.C.," continued Cameron. "They got it up there on a freight elevator." He decided to heighten the drama. "And it sat untouched for twenty years. Unused. Unloved." "Whaaat?" Zach asked, "Why would someone do that?" "I really dunno," Cameron admitted. "Weird, man," concluded Jay.

The boys—with two of them now using their phone flashlights—looked around. Zach lifted the lid of a cabinet in the back seating area. "A sink!" "Yup," said Cameron, in tour guide mode. "And it's got a fridge, a bed, and a closet. A hammock, too. It hangs from the inside ceiling." Zach could barely take it all in. "Man! When we're sixteen, let's drive this baby to California. Just the three of us. Goin' surfin'!" Jay added, "Southern California beaches... Hollywood... Movie stars! Bikini babes!" "Jay," Cameron said, "Cool your jets."

But Jay was on a roll. "Zach could sleep in the hammock, 'cause he's the shrimp." Zach retaliated, "Sure, I'll sleep in the hammock that'll be hanging inside the bus, while you sleep outside! Look out for bears, Jay." He growled and made a threatening gesture with his imaginary claws, all of which Jay considered extremely lame.

As the boys nosed around, Jay spied a tattered manila folder crammed down tight in the cranny behind the driver's seat. There was no glove box in the bus. "Here's papers. Looks like lots of old receipts. Repair papers. Wow," he said, as he came across a sheath of official documents, "I think this is the title. 1963 Volkswagen. Man, can you believe it's fifty years old? My God, this thing's as old as a pyramid." Zach replied, "Or a mummy."

Jay studied a smaller document, a Washington, D.C. vehicle registration. "Hmm, this paper's in good shape for 1971. That's forty-two years ago. The owner was Thomas Michael Post. I bet he's dead."

ADAM A. WESCHLER & SON
Auctioneers-Appraisers
United States Marshal's Sale
of
1963 Volkswagen Camper

By virtue of an Order issued by the United States District Court for the District of Columbia, Civil Action No. 181-71, in and for the District aforesaid, at the suit of United States of America vs. ONE 1963 VOLKSWAGEN CAMPER, Serial No. 2198201? registered title owner: Thomas Michael Post, to me directed, I hereby give notice that on TUESDAY, JANUARY 11, 1972, 10 A.M. I will offer for sale the aforementioned camper BY PUBLIC AUCTION, to the highest bidder for CASH (payable in currency or certified check drawn to the order of the Auxtioneer at time of sale). Sale to take place at KALORAMA GARAGE, 1649 KALORAMA RD., N.W. ANTHONY E. PAPA, United States Marshal in and for the District of Columbia

DECEMBER 24, 31 & JANUARY 7

Jay thumbed through the papers. "This is kinda weird. It says 'Notice of U.S. Marshal's sale'. So the bus was auctioned. In 1972. And sold to Harold Morders, of 14th Street in Washington, D.C."

"Murders?" Zach misheard him accidently-on-purpose. "Morders," corrected Jay. Acting like still he hadn't heard, Zach repeated, "Murders?" "No! It's Moooorders, with an "o," not murders." "Well, it *sounds* like murders," insisted Zach. "You think the guy was murdered? Maybe he or his whole family was murdered, and that's why no one wanted to use the bus, and they just stored it away. I bet it was cursed."

It was hopeless; Zach would pretty much do anything for attention. Jay returned his attention to the ancient looking papers. "What? This one says 'United States of America versus One 1963 Volkswagen Camper'. It's like the U.S. government was going after the bus like it was some kind of a criminal."

"Dang! At the auction it sold for only a hundred and seventy-five dollars. Can you believe that? A hundred and seventy-five bucks?" blurted Jay. "Well, it must have been wrecked, or involved in some crime, for it to not be worth more than that," Cameron guessed. "I dunno," said Jay. "There had to have been some reason it was being auctioned in a U.S. Marshal's sale. If you wreck your car, it just goes to the insurance company or gets fixed. It doesn't get auctioned by a U.S. Marshal."

"It was cursed," Zach maintained. "It's a *death-mobile*. People died in this thing. Man, this is gettin' creepy." Jay, now annoyed, lost it. "Scaredy-cat. Is Zachy a wittle bit scared?? Watch out Zach! There's a ghost sitting right next to you, man!"

But, by speaking without thinking, Jay had gotten close to articulating the mystery of the bus. There was something weird-feeling about being inside it, beyond it just having been abandoned for so long. Something that practically demanded the boys investigate it. They all sensed it. Cameron said, "We should check it out. Let's find out what happened. We can research it and discover its secret." "Hey, it'll be our summer project," Zach said, "and we can make a movie out of it." Jay said, exasperated, "Oh geez, Zach. You wanna make a movie out of *everything*."

"Well," said Zach, defending his track record, "I'm goin' to make movies. You should check out my YouTube videos." "Pullease...I've seen 'em, Cam showed me. Rank amateur!" "Bull! Show me what you've done, big man!"

Cameron chimed in, "Cut it out guys. Let's make a plan. What we'll do is go to that address of the original owner. We'll knock on the door and see what we can find."

"Cameron, you're a dreamer," said Jay. "Those papers are forty years old, dude. You think the family is still gonna be livin' there?"

"You just never know," Cameron said, reasonably. "Maybe whoever lives there knew them, or knows the story." "Or a neighbor might know" Zach agreed. "We could knock on the next door neighbors, too. Somebody will know the story."

"Here we come, the new-age Hardy Boys. Hardy Boys with iPhones!" said Jay. If they'd been the Three Musketeers, they'd have raised and clinked their swords. But as it was, the threesome high-fived. "Junior detectives!" said Zach. "I can see the credits now. Awesome. Disney will want this." Jay couldn't resist a put-down. "Maybe John 'Dizzie' will want it. Zach, your new 'stage name' is now gonna be Zach Dizzie. Mr. Dizzie!" "Loser," said Zach. Cameron called them back to order. *"Guys!"*

Chapter 2 – Doodle

The boys gathered around Cameron's bedroom desk, where he kept his laptop, and he typed the VW's original owner's address into Google. Cameron had wrested control of the detached mouse, and was peering intently into the screen, with the other boys crouched and crowding him from behind, like an angel and devil perched on opposite shoulders.

"Here," said, Jay, "click on that Zillow link. That'll tell us how much the house is worth. Let's see if it's a big house." Cameron scrolled down the screen as they watched, until their eyes lit on the home value statistics. "Gosh, it sold for one point five million dollars three years ago! Geez, the Post family was rich."

Jay continued to direct the search. "Go to Google Maps and let's see the street view, and check out what this place looks like." They opened Google Earth, and the Western Hemispheric globe spun into position, paused and then zeroed in on the Eastern Seaboard. Then the graphics dropped them into the D.C. Metro area, into Washington, D.C., and then to the individual city blocks. They plummeted into the frame like a parachutist.

At Jay's urging, Cameron clicked on the little yellow man icon, dragged him over, and planted him at the street address where the house was located on the graphics of the street map. "Whoa, now *that's* a nice house," Cameron said, as the building's photo came into view. Jay quickly agreed. "Big house, man. They were frozen in contemplation for a moment. What to do next? Zach spoke up. "It's pretty simple. Let's go knock on the door."

The group planned out a visit for the next morning, a Saturday, figuring that would be the best chance someone would be home. Their project, *the investigation*, had made them unusually mindful that their freeform summer schedule was not a privilege for people outside their own peer group. But something else occurred to Jay; an information trail that might provide a key to the mystery. "Hey, how rare do you think the hippie van is? Like, how many you think they made in '63?

Cameron typed in the search phrase, "Number of VW Buses built 1963." The Wikipedia result appeared at the top of the page of Google choices.

Choosing the Wiki link, Jay skimmed the page and found what he was looking for. "Cool, this even tells how they came up with the whole idea of building a VW Bus in the first place. A guy named Ben Pon was the Dutch Volkswagen importer. He had the idea and sketched it in a doodle, in 1947. And they started building buses in 1949. I would have thought they started building them in the '60s."

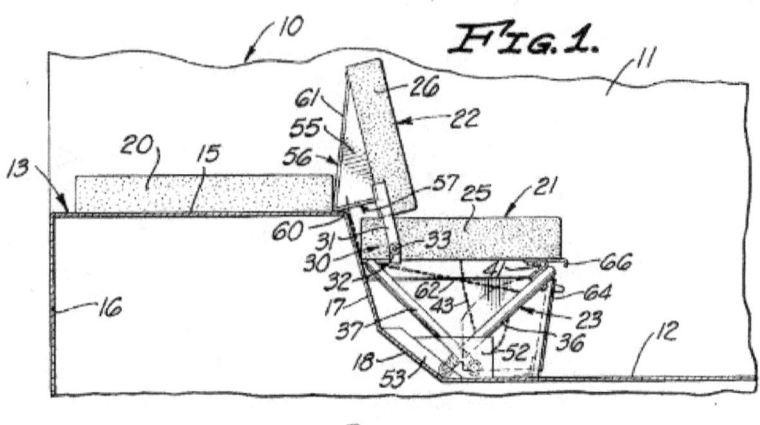

FIG. 1.

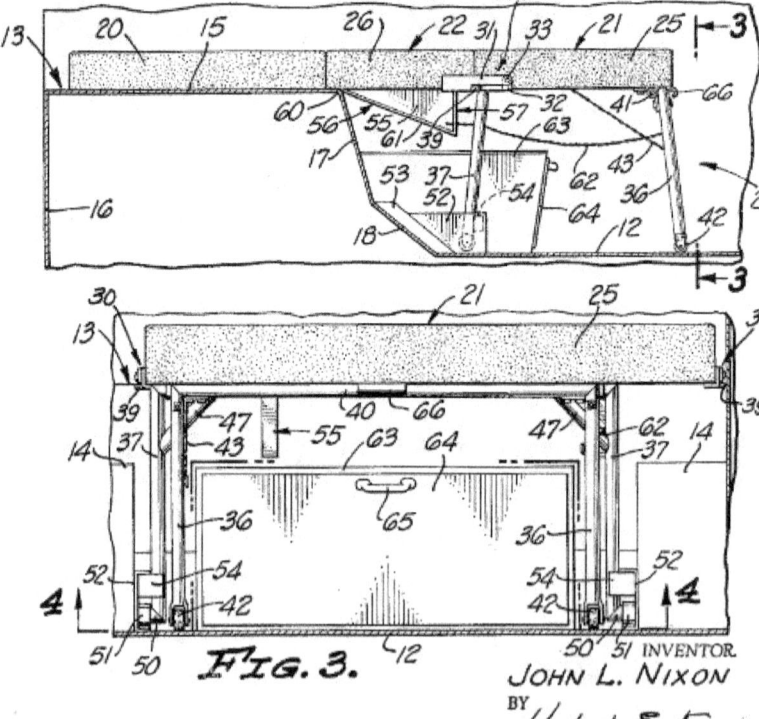

FIG. 2.

FIG. 3.

INVENTOR.

JOHN L. NIXON

BY

Herbert E. Fadder

AGENT

Jay continued to read off the page. "This chart shows that they sold thirty-eight thousand VW buses in the U.S. in 1963. That sounds like a lot. You could even get an ambulance. VW built six hundred seventy-five VW bus ambulances that year."

The first Volkswagen bus campers were created with camper 'kits', made by the German company Westfalia, beginning in 1954. By around 1960, camper conversions were also being installed in the U.S., especially in California.

Californian John Dixon was in the camper business, and is best known for his Sundial campers. In the mid-'60s his company had over one hundred employees doing conversions. John started in the business by visiting the VW dealerships and installing the camper conversions on the spot. Later, VW insisted the work be done in a factory, and so he took over an old building that'd been a skating rink. Even though the basic VW bus had windows, the campers were built using a Kombi. The Kombi had no windows, so the installer cut out the window holes and installed-windows.

In order for a Volkswagen dealer to get as many cars from the manufacturer as he could potentially sell, he also had to accept a certain amount of Kombis. By converting some of them into campers, the dealer had a much easier time selling them.

Chapter 3 – Window Bars

Saturday morning was not especially buggy or humid, and the boys each got out of their homes without having to endure much—or any—interrogation from their parents. It was usually enough for them to say that they were hanging out together, and gloss over any specifics. Actually, for the most part, they didn't strike their parents as having the desire to get up to anything illicit, so they were given free reign.

They biked across the 14th Street Bridge into D.C., rode north and pedaled uptown to their general destination, Dupont Circle, passing the hotels and restaurants that fringe of Embassy Row. They coasted down the sidewalk of a street of large homes. One of the region's main residential architectural features are row houses, with each dwelling on a block attached to the next one in line, and with linked porches, but separate entranceways. There was a particularly ornate three-story Brownstone at the 21st street address. It could have been considered a mansion. The overhang over the front stoop featured a stone post upon two columns, which was probably quite stylish for the day. Cameron could tell the other two were hesitating at the sidewalk, and so he kind of shoved them towards the front steps leading up to the porch and handsome entranceway.

Next to the solid and uninviting door of solid dark
oak was a plaque reading "Historic Preservation

Washington, D.C., Facade Donated." Cameron rang the doorbell and they waited nervously. Without delay, the big door drew open, and a petit dark-skinned lady stood in the doorway, peering at them quizzically, though not in an unfriendly way. She held a lit cigarette and waited to hear what they had to say, as they collected themselves. Cameron thought, "This is a fancy house. She could be the owner or she might be the housekeeper. I'd better act as if she's the owner, so I don't insult her." The woman continued to give the boys the once-over.

Cameron broke the ice. "Hello ma'am, we're sorry to bother you, but we're trying to find out information on someone who used to live here. We're doing research, and it has to do with a vintage car." The boys collectively recognized that this was a slightly unconventional situation, and they fought back nervousness by trying to appear purposeful.

Cameron positioned the folder in his hands to open it and show her a picture of the bus. He'd made sure to print a large photo to be able to show anyone they spoke to. This was partially because he knew people couldn't help but grin when they saw a classic VW bus, and that might take the edge off the fact that strangers were knocking at their door. The picture was one Cameron's dad had taken, and showed Cameron standing in front of the open 'barn doors' of the bus, as the side doors are called. That view also showed it was outfitted as a camper.

The lady was clearly impressed, though also a little relieved that these kids weren't just lost, or soliciting, or something. "Oh," she said, "that's quite a car." Cameron now had a foothold. "The owner of this bus lived in your house many years ago, and we're just wondering if you might know anything about him. There's a mystery about the car and its owner, and we're trying to solve it." He pulled the old vehicle registration card from the folder, and explained that it was from 1971. It showed a Thomas Michael Post once lived at this address, back in the day.

With the mention of Thomas Post, it occurred to the lady that everyone would be more comfortable if there were introductions all around. She introduced herself as Amina, and the boys responded in their turn. She searched her mind for any way that she could be of help. "The couple who sold us the house didn't say anything about that. What's the nature of the mystery?" Zach piped up, "The bus was sold by the U.S. Marshall in an auction, and then it was put away in storage for over twenty years." Jay, not to be outdone by Zach, added, "And it sat in a garage not far from here." By now, the lady at the door was sold. "Oh yes, that does sound like a mystery." She seemed to be enjoying her visitors, the three clean cut young men.

There wasn't much she could offer, but she said, "We've only lived here eight years, so I don't know much history going back to that time." It was clear that she was a relatively recent émigré, but that would be typical of the diversity of residential D.C. Cameron thought to inquire, "You've got an unusual accent, ma'am. May I ask where you're from?" Cameron had learned from watching his father meet people over the years. People liked to be asked questions like that. "Somalia." "Oh," said Cameron, conversationally. We hear a lot about Somalia in the news nowadays." All of the boys immediately thought of 'pirates,' although Zach let his mind wander a little further out, and he free-associated, and thought 'goblins.' He fidgeted a little bit, and Jay had to elbow him in the side. The lady, not put on the spot at all regarding news of pirates, agreed, "Yes, you do. Some good, and some not so good."

Cameron decided to get back to the topic at hand. "Could I ask you if your home has a garage?" "It has a parking area out back," Amina said. The boys had visualized a dedicated garage. But considering they lived in less cramped quarters in Virginia, they hadn't reckoned on the value placed on parking availability of *any* kind in the city. Cameron said, "Oh, I was hoping there might be a garage where the bus once lived."

Amina offered, "There's a man across the street you could ask. His name is Paul, and I think he's lived here twenty-eight years. His is the black door, and there's a chair next to the door, where he used to sit out in front. I'm about to go out." That might have explained why she opened the door so quickly when they rang the doorbell.

They walked with Amina, down the sidewalk and around back to the parking area, to check out where the bus might have been parked years ago. And then they thanked her and headed for the neighbor's house. Paul's front door was another substantial mass of dark, heavy wood. But in front of that door was a set of iron bars, much like a jail cell door. This was a common sight in older Washington, D.C. homes. It was one way for you to leave your front door open and still have your house be secure. Cameron looked down at the bottom of this outer door, and saw a lockbox attached to one of the bars. These were commonly used by real estate agents, but along with the darkness of the house, these two factors might indicate that Paul had moved or passed away, and the house was in transition. Cameron hoped not. If Paul was dead, he wouldn't be much help; their trail would have hit a wall. The boys had brought some Post-Its and tape, and they left a note on Paul's door. "We are looking for information on a neighbor going back to 1971. His name was Thomas Michael Post, and he owned a VW bus. If you know anything about him, please call Cameron." And Cameron included his cell number, not that he made too many phone calls. His communication-style tended more towards texting and Instagram.

"Let's take a quick spin by Weschler's," said Cameron. "Westers?" asked Zach. "Weschler's. It's the auction house that did the bus auction. I've been there before, with my dad. It's across the street from the FBI headquarters. Let's see if they can give us any info about the bus. It's worth a shot."

They cruised across town on their bikes. When they arrived at the stately building where auctions have been held weekly for one hundred and twenty years, they needed to secure their bikes. Being in the shadow of the neighboring FBI building was no guarantee their bikes would be safe. A mixed urban neighborhood—swarming with tourists, riff raff, hipsters and business 'suits'—had grown up around the venerable auction house.

The FBI edifice is the closest thing in Washington to a prop from a *Star Wars* movie. Towering over the neighboring buildings, and with no windows at street level, it casts an ominous tone. It's slated for demolition, not because of any condition issues, but because it is so damn unfriendly to humankind. The plan is for it to be replaced with something that can accommodate retail storefronts and sidewalk cafes, and classy offices or high-end condos on the upper floors.

The boys finally succeeded in securing the one bike lock around three bikes and a street lamp pole. They leapt up Weschler's front stairs and into the elevator lobby. It was almost time to start heading home for dinner. The directory indicated that the offices were on the third floor, and so they boarded the elevator. The elevator operator looked like he'd worked there almost as long as they'd been in the auction business. But he was a very friendly guy. He probably knew all the regulars.

The boy detectives exited for the office, banked a left, and faced a tall counter. "May I help you?" asked an apparently suspicious receptionist. Weschler's didn't usually have unaccompanied children as visitors.

"Yes ma'am. We're investigating...uh, I mean *researching*, an auction. In 1972 you all auctioned off an old Volkswagen bus. Here's a picture of it, and here's a copy of the auction notice..."

Weschler's also didn't have too many people inquiring about auctions from forty years ago. "What are you trying to find out, gentlemen?" "Well, we're trying to find out why this bus was auctioned. If there was a lawsuit, or a crime, or what?" asked Cameron.

"I'm sorry. We really don't have records going back that far," she said, with a tone that implied that she would rather die than allow a breach of confidentiality. Cameron suspected that somewhere in this cavernous old building, records probably still existed that went back that far. But he could tell that he wasn't going to have much luck getting someone to search for him.

Chapter 4 - eBay

On Sunday, the boys decided to take another look at the bus to see if they'd missed anything. Since it had a closet, and narrow cabinet doors, they carefully checked inside the cavities of those areas. Also, the bed and seat cushions were designed to be lifted up, which allowed them to look underneath. With all three of them burrowing around, in each other's way, the bus felt confining but also somehow accommodating.

Jay said, "I found a peace sign!" and flashed them a two-fingered peace sign. Zach, now hyperaware that *he* hadn't found anything cool yet, asked, "Where?" "It was right here, on the floor of the closet, and it's on a gold chain. Looks kinda cheap, but I bet it's old." Feeling the need to supervise the operation, Cameron said, "Let's lift this bed cushion up and look around under it." Zach followed Cameron's cue, in his own manner, "I'm going to look under the dashboard." Jay objected, "The dashboard! What in the world do you think you'll find under the dash? Somebody's old chewing gum?" Zach answered with uncommon objectivity, "You never know. It's dark under here and there's a bunch of wires, but not as many as a regular car would have. This is one simple machine."

Zach twisted and turned, with his head under the dash and at an angle. He was trying to get his hands into a compressed space; it wasn't the first time his being small came in handy. When he was younger, and his mom forgot her keys, he could get in the house through the doggie door. There was a little paper strip of some kind wedged up in the crevice where the dash attached to the inner chassis. He wasn't sure he could get it out. But, after a few tries, out it came.

Zach, having finally freed it, held it aloft. "Look at this. It's a fake ticket to a Beatles concert. Pretty neat, huh?" Jay's mental wheels began to spin. "Let me see that. Are you sure it's fake? Remember, this is a 1963 bus and the ticket says 1964. It could be real."

Cameron wondered what it was doing under the dashboard. "You know, based on where you seem to have found it, Zach," said Jay, "I think it could have been stuck up on top of the dash, and slipped down behind it. This ticket could be authentic. My dad's a music fanatic. I can ask him."

Cameron saw an opportunity come into focus. There was money to be made. "If it's real, we could sell it on eBay."

The boys would later think back on, and try to replay this moment, to try and understand whether they should have considered another course of action. Their adventures together had a life and logic all their own; this thing—the sudden appearance of the ticket and the urge to sell it—was just one of those ideas that 'made sense at the time.' Not that the impulse to cash in was unanimous.

Zach put in, "Cameron, it's your Dad's. It was in his bus." Cam was unwavering; he didn't especially like to be challenged by Zach, the youngest. "Nahhh. If we find some junk on the floor, he won't care if we keep it. I don't think he'd care about an old concert ticket, even if it's the Beatles."

Jay decided that if the others disagreed, it was his turn to mediate. "I'll show it to my Dad tonight." That would take care of any hassles over ticket authenticity, or over 'finders' keepers,' versus 'possession being nine-tenths of the law.' Cameron remained starry-eyed. "If this thing is real, it could be worth a thousand bucks. We'd each get, umm...three hundred, thirty-three dollars and thirty-three cents."

They were all thinking it, even if Cameron was the one to say it, "Money for a piece of paper you can't even use anymore to get into a concert? A *lot* of money?" He added, "That would be *sweet!*"

"Let's go by Velocity Co-op, so I can check out the banana bike again. Maybe now I'm really going to be able to get it," said Cam. Down the Avenue at Velocity, there was always a row of used bikes for sale in a rack out front. If you wanted to do your own bike repairs, you could use all their tools for a small fee.

"Why would you want one of those?" inquired Zach, "You got a nice new bike; absolutely has to be a much faster ride then a kid's bike from the '70s."

"It's awesome. Have you seen the gear shifter on it?" said Cam, and they tooled on down Mount Vernon Avenue to the bright orange storefront. An old ten-speed jutted out of the upper façade to identify it as a bike shop. There were big decorative wings on the walls where the bike frame was mounted, to look as if they sprouted from the bike, like Victoria's Secret angels.

Chapter 5 – No Reserve

Jay phoned Cameron and said his dad was confident the ticket was the real deal, and actually could be worth a thousand dollars. Cameron figured Jay's dad would know if anyone did. Whereas some people had a wall of books in their den, Jay's dad had an entire wall of CDs and vinyl LPs. All perfectly sorted and organized. It was no-touch territory for Jay and his sister. He fastidiously rotated his music library on his iPod, so his jogs included a constant variety of music.

The ticket was faded pink, maybe it had originally been red. Today's concert tickets are glossy and include bar codes and holograms. This ticket looked like a small section rectangle of colored construction paper, like we remember from grade school. Black block letters spelled out 'WASHINGTON COLISEUM, 3rd & M STS, N.E., WASHINGTON, D.C.' Time and day was spelled out 'TUE. EVE. FEB. 11, 1964, 8:00 P.M.' The section, row and seat numbers were there. The printer company was listed, along with tiny logo you used to see on the edge of campaign buttons; in this case for the printers union in New York City. The largest letters were 'THE BEATLES' and the ticket cost was 'Est. Price $3.73, Fed. Tax .27, Total $4.00.'

Cameron could sense Jay's excitement over the phone. "Jay, can your dad help put it on eBay?" "Sure," Jay responded, but also hesitated a moment, "Do you think we should?" "Let's go for it. There's a bike with my name on it."

It didn't take long to set up the eBay listing. Jay's dad— accepting some vague assurance from Jay that Cameron's dad *knew* what the boys were up to, or thinking that's what he heard his son to say—took a nice close-up photo of the front and back of the ticket, and they did the eBay listing together.

There were decisions to be made. Would it be an actual auction, as opposed to a 'buy-it-now'? Would there be a minimum reserve price set? Jay's dad recommended they go with an actual auction. This way the market would determine the final price, and it left open the possibility of it bringing a high price. Offering it at no reserve would send an important message. "No games being played; this object is really for sale." The boys agreed with his suggestions, and the opening price was set at one dollar. If it ended up selling for a disappointing price, well, no real harm done. It was a found object anyway. On the other hand, starting it at a buck would serve to tempt more bidders to get in on the action. A high starting price might scare off some bidders. And bidders who got in early were likely to become mentally invested, and decide to stick with the auction even if it went beyond where they hoped the price would ascend. The boys understood there was a psychological strategy necessary when placing an item for auction on eBay.

Within a few hours, the bidding was up to two hundred and ten dollars.

Chapter 6 – Solicitation

Five days later, the boys were little more than thirty-six hours away from being "rich." The ticket had been bid up to seven hundred and eighty dollars, and would probably go higher based on the number of bidders. By clicking on the link showing the number of bids, you could see that there had been eight bidders so far.

Each boy had already planned out exactly how they would spend their share.

Of course, with eBay, there was always a potential for a last minute pop. As automated bidding services had become more and more widely used, there were sometimes gargantuan leaps in bidding in the last few seconds. This isn't something you can predict, but it's always a possibility with a rare and desirable object.

Cam checked his phone for Instagram updates, as he did several times a day. This time he decided to also check for voicemails, which he hardly ever did. For the first six months he had an iPhone, he didn't even set up voicemail. The kids nowadays just didn't use it. This time there were two messages, certainly both spam to be quickly deleted. He checked anyway, and one of the messages was actually a follow-up to a birthday party invitation, and the other was a solicitation. He thought of how much he hated those junk calls. Someday he hoped they'd be illegal.

Before he had a chance to hit delete, his mom called up at him from downstairs. Dinner time. He put down the phone and headed for the stairs. His leg reached down for that first step, but his mind pulled it back. He spun around and headed back into the bedroom. That spam caller had identified himself as "Paul." Could it be the Paul from Saturday's 14th Street investigation, who was evidently now *not* dead?

Cam listened to the message, growing excited as he took it in, like he'd aimed at a difficult target and *hit* it. *Bullseye!* "Hello. I'm Paul. You asked me to give you a call, and so I am. Yes, I know something about Mr. Post that I'd be willing to share. Call me." And he left his number.

Without hesitation, Cam dialed. Paul answered, and Cam introduced himself. Then, he told Paul about how they were trying to find out the story of the bus, and find out why it was auctioned and then not used for twenty years. Excited and unable to help himself, Cameron went into 'too much information' mode. "We actually found an old Beatles concert ticket in the bus, and we're selling it on eBay." Immediately he wished he hadn't mentioned that to Paul, who was essentially a total stranger. The ticket auction wasn't even common knowledge within his *own* family. Cameron thought, "Me and my big mouth. Sometimes I don't know when to stop talking."

Even though Cam would have felt better taking his statement back, Paul seemed particularly attentive. He asked, "Hold on! Has it been sold?"

Cameron, starting to feel like he was in over his head, clarified, "The ticket?" To which Paul answered, "Yes." "The auction closes tomorrow." Paul sounded weirdly intense. "You'd better come and see me. Can you come by my house in the morning?" "Why?" Paul offered no explanation beyond, "I have something to tell you before you do anything rash. It's important. Come at ten."

Cam phoned the guys, and they planned their visit to see Paul, their 'informant.' He thought, "Things are happening pretty fast!" He was also conscious of something harder to express; the excitement of wanting to know more about something, to uncover a secret.

Chapter 7 – Rotunda

The boys wheeled up to Paul's, knocked on the front door, and waited. Finally he opened the wooden door, and then the metal bar door, and welcomed them. A mild mannered looking fellow, and a bit disheveled in his attire; his skin had that 'I've spent many summers on the beach' look. "Welcome, guys." He led the threesome into his cluttered living room. With twenty-eight years in one house, the interior decoration-style approached 'junior hoarder.' In Paul's case, it was mostly geegaws strewn around except one stand out item of the décor. On his main wall, he displayed a large photo of the U.S. Capitol. Within its simple institutional looking white-washed wooden frame, it spanned more than four feet.

THE CAPITOL
1860

The black and white image was clearly old; the huge building's rotunda was evidently still under construction. While the building was the focus of the composition, there was what looked to be a canal in the foreground, in what would probably be called the lawn. Then there was a canal starting at the bottom of the photo border and going right up to the Capitol. A canal, with locks and all. And pathways along the water's edge for mules or other livestock to pull the barges. As the boys all stared at the photo, Jay recalled hearing the builders of the Capitol did at one time rely on a canal to haul in the building materials.

Paul directed them to the couch, and he took a wingback chair facing them. He made them feel at ease; they felt as though he regarded them as adults, and that they could speak openly about important things.

Paul gestured towards the vintage photo; it took up much of the space on the wall dividing the living room from the kitchen area. It riveted the boys' attention. "Thomas was my neighbor, and he was a friend. We were never very close, but I don't think

Thomas had any close friends. That photo of the U.S. Capitol, it was his. The Architect of the Capitol gave it to him. It had hung in some back hallway for years. Thomas loved working at the Capitol, more than anything. Well, that and his bus."

"I was surprised to hear that your dad has the bus Thomas owned. I can hardly believe it still exists. Always wondered what became of it. I figured it'd gone to the crusher years ago."

"Well, let me start at the beginning."

Chapter 8 – Yellowstone

Thomas Post was the quiet 'black sheep' in his family. Since the family was relatively well to do, he could have attended just about any college. But Thomas was not really aspirational in his youth. His family was from the east, but he'd gone to Northern California because of its new frontier-ish, progressive culture.

He'd never been close to any family members, and this only succeeded in making him seem to be more of an outcast. One line of the family had considerable wealth, but it didn't reach over into his lineage. None of that mattered to Thomas. So Thomas became a bit of a nature boy.

He was in tune with the political idealism of the day, with the youthful and brash Kennedy administration especially capturing his imagination. He started to become attracted to the world of government in those idealistic times, and Washington, D.C. was his new dream destination.

So, his plan was to relocate to the Nation's Capital, and find employment as close as he could to the presidential administration that he now so admired. He read that there were lots of jobs in the support staff of the Senate and the House. That would allow expression for his 'public-spirited' side. Thomas was a bright guy, but pretty much a loner. He decided he'd like to head for the East Coast, but he'd take his time and see the country and its natural wonders en route, and then settle down in D.C. He resolved to visit as many national parks as possible, on his cross-country journey to Washington.

He could save money during the trip by sleeping in his vehicle. Looking around at the options, he found the Volkswagen campers were often equipped with a bed, kitchen table, sink, clothes closet and a refrigerator. Thus equipped, he'd have little need for hotel rooms.

A small trust fund enabled him to afford a brand new green and white VW camper. With his new bus, Thomas was ready to head out. But first, he studied up on national parks to plot out his trip.

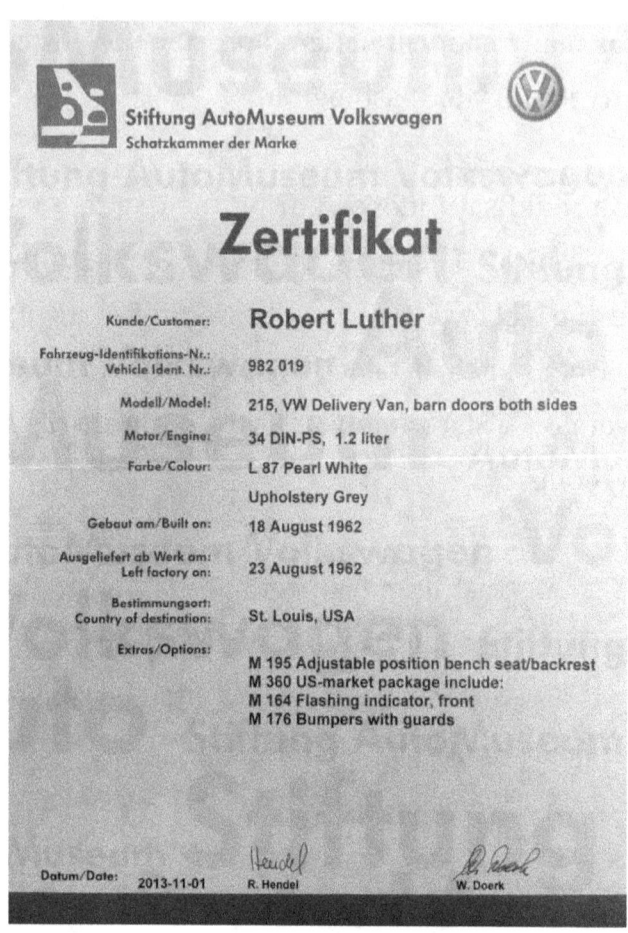

Stiftung AutoMuseum Volkswagen
Schatzkammer der Marke

Zertifikat

Kunde/Customer:	**Robert Luther**
Fahrzeug-Identifikations-Nr.: Vehicle Ident. Nr.:	982 019
Modell/Model:	215, VW Delivery Van, barn doors both sides
Motor/Engine:	34 DIN-PS, 1.2 liter
Farbe/Colour:	L 87 Pearl White
	Upholstery Grey
Gebaut am/Built on:	18 August 1962
Ausgeliefert ab Werk am: Left factory on:	23 August 1962
Bestimmungsort: Country of destination:	St. Louis, USA
Extras/Options:	
	M 195 Adjustable position bench seat/backrest
	M 360 US-market package include:
	M 164 Flashing indicator, front
	M 176 Bumpers with guards

Datum/Date:	2013-11-01	R. Hendel	W. Doerk

Thomas planned a June 1963 departure, and then to travel through the summer—when the mountain passes in upper Yosemite were clear of snow—with the intent to make it to Washington, D.C. by the fall. He'd head east from San Francisco, in an almost straight line, to Yosemite.

Yosemite, his first stop, was a tremendous experience with its magnificent lakes and cliffs, and the awesome Mariposa Sequoia Grove. On the downside, there were the mosquitoes. He stuck to the campgrounds, with communal showers, dotting the valley. At night, he had multiple options. The bus was outfitted with a cot, a bed, and a hammock. If he chose the cot, he would erect the tent which could be affixed to the side of the bus.

When it was time to leave California, he pointed the bus in the direction of Yellowstone, Thomas' most anticipated stop, because of the many photos of the geyser Old Faithful he'd seen. He traveled diagonally up through Nevada, north on 395 and then followed Route 80 into Southern Idaho. The route featured extensive plots of desert; endless miles of Indian reservations withering in the heat, dust devils, and smoke from distant range fires as he rode past. Traversing Idaho, the landscape featured scrubby greenery, and the occasional aspen and stands of Lodgepole Pines, amid the rock formations.

Particularly interesting and strange were the massive bales of hay, lying like horizontal silos along the expanse of farmland. Motoring along, he was frequently passed by motorcyclists without helmets. The days passed contentedly during his Yellowstone stay. West Yellowstone featured the largest geothermal volcano in the Western Hemisphere. Thomas camped outside at an old railroad worker compound near a lodge and a cluster of log cabins and teepees. The VW bus was welcome anywhere there was a small clearing.

Thomas would have to drive far to the North, but Glacier National Park was a must. One of his dreams was to walk upon a real glacier. On Going-to-the-Sun-Road, a black bear sprinted out right in front of the bus before bounding down the slope below.

Chapter 9 – Hartnett Hall

And so the weeks passed. The bus puttered through the expanses of rolling green farmland in Ohio and Pennsylvania during the last day of the trip, and the interstate signage began the count-down to his destination. Upon Thomas' arrival in Washington, D.C.—which represented quite an adjustment from being ensconced in national parks to a regimented, low-rise urban setting—his first item of business was to find housing. The local paper had many rooms for rent, but the gas station attendant suggested Hartnett Hall Boarding Complex, on 14th Street.

If you look up and down the block today, you'll see some of the most beautiful Brownstones and townhouses in Washington. In the 1950s through the 1970s, it was all owned by one man, John Hartnett, and every house was divided into small rooms. Each unit had just enough room for a sink and a bed. Somewhere on each floor was a shared bathroom, its location defined by its original location when it was a single family home. The rooms usually measured nine by six feet. Each building was considered a 'dorm,' with some for men and some for women.

It was a popular destination for young people who were moving to Washington, D.C to work for the federal government. For ten dollars a week, you got your room, maid service, and two meals a day. At the end of the block was a dining hall that would seat one hundred and twenty. In addition to this block, other buildings in this area were part of it and added up to eight hundred rooms, all close to Dupont Circle. Many of these homes were originally beautiful mansions. The house that Paul currently lived in had at one time been broken up into forty rooms, as part of the Hartnett Hall complex. Thomas occupied a room in the house right across the street. As the area began to gentrify, the homes were sold off and converted back to single family homes. A stroke of financial luck enabled Paul to go from being a tenant in his building, to acquiring it, in its entirety, as his home.

Thomas liked the house his room was in, because of its moody architecture and where his room was located. You can see still see today how distinctive his building was, with its oval hooded front porch. Thomas was smitten with the home before he'd even walked through the door. He secured a room on the third floor, in the back. The backside of his building was also perfect, because he could keep an eye on his bus, parked in its own spot.

Once he was situated, Thomas pounded the pavement looking for a job. And not just any job, Thomas yearned to work in Congress, in the great cavernous rooms where the law of the land was debated and voted on. And it worked out just like that, with him landing a job as a janitor at the U.S. Capitol Building. Pushing a broom, or wielding a mop, alongside men who represented thousands of constituents...this was a dream come true for Thomas. He was now close to the action, just as he'd imagined.

Chapter 10 – Fabergé

Thus settled in, the time had come for Thomas to pay a visit to his Great Aunt Marjorie. Marjorie Merriweather Post was the doyenne of the 'old money' branch of Thomas' relations; a gracious, if distant, part of his extended family. By this time, he'd been to some of the grand houses and museums in town, and thought it would be a shame if he didn't extend himself and visit. It would be a neighborly gesture. It was only right for him to call on her.

He decided that it might be best to just show up; he had to admit, honestly, that her wealth and grandeur was intimidating. Even with their family connection, he anticipated feeling out of place. He overcame his cold feet by reasoning that if he just showed up, she couldn't say 'no' to his visit. So, he just took off with his local road map, navigating the winding, leafy hills of Northwest Washington. He drove into her neighborhood, one of the finest and most upscale in the Nation's Capital. As he approached her home, named Hillwood, he could tell from his map that he was on a crest of a hill over Rock Creek Park. Rock Creek Park runs though the District of Columbia in a pattern that looks like a many branched oak tree when it's seen on a wall map. The entranceway was imposing, and '*Drat!*' there was a guard. It was clearly hard to be spontaneous when mingling with high society.

"Mr. Thomas Post to visit Mrs. Post, please." he almost shouted at the guard in the gatehouse. 'Oh, well,' he thought. That's what came of his attempt to act 'nonchalant.' "Just a moment sir." And, with that, the guard picked up his phone. After a minute, the gates swung open and the guard motioned in the direction of the house. Thomas pulled in and swung around the circular drive. He stepped down from the drivers' seat, paced a bit, and looked around. Boy, he thought, the bus looked good in front of the imposing house. O.K., anything would look good in front of that. He headed for the front door. He knocked with a weighty brass knocker, and a butler swung open one of the massive doors. "Mrs. Post will be see you in the parlor," motioning the way. Thomas thanked him. He entered the parlor, and sat down in a Victorian couch.

When Mrs. Post entered the room, she looked almost like she was arriving for a formal ball, with part of her gown in a train, following her on the floor. Her great fortune was derived from breakfast cereal. When her father had passed away, she became the sole owner of the Postum Cereal Company. However, nothing in her manner indicated that Mrs. Post was anything other than the warmest possible hostess. Everyone was made to feel most welcome in her presence. "Hello, Thomas," she said, as if he was expected. "It's good of you to visit. What are you making of yourself these days?" "I work in the U.S. Capitol, ma'am." "That's marvelous, Thomas."

They sat a while and talked, and the time passed slowly. Another Mrs. Post, Emily Post (no relation), the writer of books on etiquette and comportment, had no doubt proscribed the exact minimum amount of time for a hostess to indulge a well-meaning but uninvited guest. That time was fast approaching. Thomas' Great Aunt seemed bored with him. She was a woman of the world, a great collector of decorative arts, and her home featured some of the finest treasures in the world. Her collection of Russian Fabergé included Catherine the Great's Easter Egg. Only about forty of the Fabergé Easter Eggs were ever made, and all were for members of the Russian Royal

Family before they met an unfortunate and violent end in the revolutionary uprising.

Thomas knew he should make a big deal out of this showplace, but he was not a lover of beauty or aesthetics so removed from practical purpose, so he didn't seem to pay much attention to the surroundings. The visit wore on, with the clock in the great marble hall ticking along in the distance. After a little family small talk and remembrances, and a couple of extended silence, his time was up. She got up to walk him out, and they got to the front door. Her butler opened it wide and Mrs. Post decided to step out on the porch to send off Thomas with a goodbye.

And then she spied his bus. "Is that your car?" she said. "It's actually a bus. Or, technically, it's a camper." Now, she was impressed. "My, my...a camper! You mean you can camp out in it? Under the stars? In the altogether?" "Yes ma'am," Thomas confirmed. "I drove it cross country and visited several national parks. Every night was spent in the camper."

She asked his permission to inspect the vehicle. And he, of course, assented. Then the two proceeded down the walkway to where Thomas had parked.

"This is lovely!" Mrs. Post was starting to think that Thomas actually did have some sense of style, after all. This bus in a smart combination of dark green and white was fairly swanky, she thought.

She was taken with a wicked impulse. "Thomas, could you take me for a ride in it?" Thomas was nonplused, and wasn't sure he heard her right. But he was happy to accommodate. "Certainly ma'am."

As he opened the passenger door and she attempted to climb up inside, there was a scuffle from her front door. Three staff members came running out towards the bus scattering the gravel. Her Security Director, in a black suit, hollered, "Mrs. Post, ma'am! May I ask what is going on?" "Yes Jenkins," she said, calmly, but resolutely. "I'm off for a ride. I'll be just fine. Besides, Thomas is relations. He's my great nephew."

The Security Director wasn't known for his flexibility. The lady of the house entering an unauthorized vehicle set alarms off in his head. It was a breach of...*something*. Propriety, if not security as such. He had to improvise. "But ma'am, at least I should accompany you." "Don't be absurd Jenkins. It's just a quick ride around the block."

Even a broader-minded individual would have considered her assurance trifling and imprecise; the terrain was pretty spread out, with surrounding hills full of blind alleys, and so the area could hardly be considered to be parceled out into *blocks*. "Ma'am, we don't...." he continued, at a loss. "I'll be right back!" she called out brightly. What fun!

And she slammed her door. Thomas hopped in and they tooted down the drive and out onto Linnean Street. Marjorie directed him to turn left on Tilden Lane and the road descended into the park. "Turn left onto Beach Drive!" she directed. And they were now sailing down the winding road, under a dense canopy of tree limbs, just eating up the road as it wound through Rock Creek Park. If anyone did pay attention to the bus in the park that day, with the elderly woman gleefully enjoying her ride, with her face as much out of the sliding passing window as possible...would they ever have guessed that it was none other than the richest woman in America?

After fifteen minutes of cruising, Marjorie directed Thomas back to her neighborhood. Now there were five staff members out front of her home, fretting about her departure.

As they parted, Mrs. Post said, "Thomas, you're welcome to visit me anytime! And thank you so much for the ride." And at that, her security director opened the door and helped her step down from the bus.

Chapter 11 – Park & Shop

There was snow on the ground in Washington on February 9th, 1964. Thomas was running Sunday errands, and maneuvered his bus into a parking spot at the Park & Shop on Connecticut Avenue. He was surprised Jimmie's was open on a Sunday, and he went in and got a haircut. Then he picked up some items at the Sanitary Grocery Co. and returned to the bus.

Somebody had stuck a paper on his windshield. With all the icy slush on the pavement, he figured he must have missed the warning on the pavement and parked in an illegal spot. Luckily, no ticket. He grabbed the paper off the windshield, making an effort to scoot out of there as fast as possible. As he drove through the parking lot towards the exit onto

Connecticut Avenue, he noticed a frantic looking woman in his rear view mirror. She was running in the snow, and appeared to be wearing high heels! She was apparently determined to catch up to Thomas's departing bus, which was disorienting. The moment she arrived outside his door, she rapped on his window, even though his face was just inches behind the glass. He reached up and slid the driver's window open. "I'm very sorry. With the ice and snow, I didn't realize I'd parked in a bad spot." He figured she must be the manager of the Park & Shop, perturbed at his parking infraction.

She seemed pretty intent, if slightly out of breath; he wasn't sure what else to say that would appease her. "Wait!" she said. "Didn't you see my note? I just want to hire you!" Thomas wasn't sure what he was hearing, and not for the first time since he'd arrived in the city. "Whhaat?" She drew a breath and explained. It so happens she needed him to ferry some people in the bus, and she was willing to pay for the service.

This didn't factor into his plans at all. Did she somehow have the wrong person? Would it conflict with his job at the Capitol? "Look, my name is Mary Sparks, and I'm with Capitol Promotions." She gave him her business card. "I just need you to take my clients to a concert on Tuesday evening. You'd just pick them up at the Shoreham Hotel and take them to the Washington Coliseum. It's your bus I'm interested in. I want to provide them with a spiffy ride to the concert.

"Seriously?" "Absolutely," said Miss Sparks, and I'll pay you cash up front. I just need you to show up at the Shoreham Hotel." She gave him directions; it was fairly close to where they were. I just need you to show up there at five p.m. Tuesday. Can you do that?" Thomas said he guessed he could. Miss Sparks took his phone number and made final arrangements. "O.K., wonderful. I'll call you Monday evening to confirm the time." Thomas finally went on his way, carefully driving through the slush.

Monday evening, right on cue, Miss Sparks phoned Thomas. She reviewed the plan. Her clients would be at the Shoreham Hotel, and Thomas should pull up to the front door at five p.m. He would then drive them over to the Washington Coliseum, a few blocks north of Mass Avenue and Union Station. Drop them off and go! That was it. The whole trip from the Shoreham to the Coliseum was less than four miles. This was a sweet deal for Thomas; some big spender paying him well for less than twenty minutes worth of work.

On Tuesday, Washington was still an icy white landscape. Thomas left work early and inched his way through the slow-moving traffic towards the Shoreham. He wanted to make absolutely sure that he was early. Not just on time, but early. No use risking the loss of his big payday by being late.

Chapter 12 – Shoreham

He pulled into the wide driveway of the handsome hotel. The Shoreham was built in 1930 and has hosted many U.S. Presidents. On March 4th, 1933, the first inaugural ball of President Franklin D. Roosevelt was held at the hotel. It's perched like a bulwark on a commanding rise overlooking Rock Creek Park.

As Thomas rounded the circle at the front entrance, he found the sidewalk area was swamped with people. And then he realized they were almost all young women. And it was noisy. He stopped, shut off the bus, and waited. Before he knew it, there was Miss Sparks rapping on his passenger side window. He reached over to twist the handle and unlock the door for her. As was typical for her, she seemed out of breath. "Hello Thomas! And thank you for coming. They are really going to enjoy this. Now, here's your payment." And she thrust her hand his way, with a bunch of twenty-dollar bills coming out of her fist.

"They'll be out in just a few minutes. Just make sure that you go straight to the Coliseum. No stops. Could we possibly close your curtains? They like privacy." Thomas didn't even consider the possibility of stopping along the way. Why would he? After a moment, he realized he was falling behind on Miss Sparks instructions. Oh, yeah, curtains. "O.K., I can un-lash the curtains." "Fine, please do so and I'll be back." And with that, she disappeared into the loud crowd. Thomas thought they were especially noisy, considering it was mostly young ladies.

After a few minutes, the noise from the crowd increased to a roar, and Thomas strained to peer through the crowd, and see what in the world was going on. A standard black limousine had just parked closely to a side entrance, and a tight phalanx of Sheraton doormen and security police were apparently in the act of escorting someone—or several people—into the open door of the passenger section. A few of the doormen held black umbrellas to shield whomever it was being escorted from view. In the rush and confusion, a majority of the screaming girls rushed the limo.

The limo pulled away, some determined girls ran to keep up with it as it gained speed. It was, however, a decoy vehicle. The bus would be the actual conveyance for the object of the girls' affection.

At that very moment, Mary was at the door and opening the back doors, the bus barn doors, for her clients. Commenting on the fake-out, and the crazed fans who'd been taken in by the ruse, she said, "Like a dog running after a car. Do they have any idea what they'd do if they caught it?" It was all overwhelming for Thomas, as his riders—who'd simply walked over to the bus in full view—piled into the back, and the inhuman roar from the crowd became deafening. Miss Sparks had to lean all the way into the passenger side door to tell Thomas that she'd be tailing the VW in a follow-car. And now the crowd seemed to be quickly growing, surging in the direction of his bus to the point where they were actually surrounded. Miss Sparks, her voice raised above the ruckus, yelled out "O.K., go!" and slapped the back of the bus, indicating that Thomas depart in haste. Nerve-wracked, Thomas followed his instructions, and inched forward, trying to break free and narrowly avoiding plowing down a young woman in his path.

For a few minutes, everyone was silent, and Thomas route. It occurred to Thomas that he had failed to even ask how many passengers he was going to have. In the dark, and the rush of it all, it looked like he had three young men. Or possibly four. Whatever the case, there were a bunch of fidgety bodies behind him, out of the frame of his rearview mirror, and thus his line of sight. In any case, he needed to focus on the road, on the brake lights of the driver in front of him. This would be enough to occupy his attention, certainly. Except that one of his passengers was reaching forward to tug at his sleeve.

"Mate!" "Hey, mate!" For some reason, there was a young British male speaking to him from behind.

Thomas didn't want to turn his head and avert his gaze, but he acknowledged the voice. "May I help you in some way?" "Mate! We'd like to stop and get some Dr. Pepper. Do you know of a place?" "I think we'll pass a High's. They should have Dr. Pepper." "O.K. mate, that'll be fine."

Thomas thought about how Mary had said not to stop, but he figured the client was the boss. They came to a High's Dairy Store along the route and Thomas pulled over. One of the passengers fiddled with the side door until he figured out how to open it, and jumped out. "Back in a jif!"

Moments later, he saw his passenger exiting the High's, with a case of soda. This person got to the bus and climbed in. The others cheered and expressed their happiness upon seeing the goods. Then a door latch rattled behind him. "Might this be a fridge? Could we stow some of this in here for later?"

Chapter 13 – Coliseum

The venue of the show was the Washington Coliseum, located hard along the railroad tracks, just a stone's throw north of Union Station.

The Coliseum was also known as the Uline Ice Arena. At age sixteen, Mike Uline was a Dutch immigrant to the United States. By the time he was twenty-one, he owned an ice plant that supplied households with refrigeration prior to Freon.

Eventually he had thirty ice plants spread throughout the Midwest.

In 1931 he moved to the Washington, D.C. area to establish a plant. Ten years later, he expanded and added an ice arena next door, for use in sporting events. This was a logical move once someone had the means to create; ice hockey had become a very popular sport.

The Uline Arena, built in 1940-1941, is considered an important building for several reasons. The building design incorporates a concrete barrel roof, with exterior ribs, and so it's very distinctive. The basic look was originated by German engineers in the 1920s, and is called the Zeiss-Dywidag system. The architect was Joseph Lapish, and was called a "master of the unusual shell concrete construction." The construction company had previously built a similar dome in 1934 for New York's Hayden Planetarium. The result is a very thin, but strong, concrete shell which allows for wide open indoor spaces.

The building played a key part in protests over segregation in the 1940s. The building was also significant in the history of segregation in Washington, D.C. African Americans were allowed to attend boxing matches, but could not purchase tickets for hockey games, figure skating shows, or other cultural events. Ultimately there were boycotts of the Arena, starting in 1943.

And it was the site of The Beatles first U.S. concert.

A flank of police and uniformed guards had motioned Thomas and the bus to a service entrance at the beginning of the event. His passengers had already disembarked. Now Miss Sparks instructed him to reconnoiter there—in that spot—afterwards. She gave him a complementary pair of tickets, and apologized for the short notice, saying that her office was up in arms last week, and she trusted that he'd already gotten a chance to ask a girlfriend or guest to meet him at The Coliseum. "Again, sorry to inconvenience you. We really fooled them back at the hotel," she gloated. Then, she disappeared into the building.

The four musicians were on a platform in the center of the floor, with the audience seated right up to the edge of the performance space, only separated by their idols by a thin blue line of policemen. The unearthly high-pitched screaming of females (and some of the male fans, as well,) was continual, although it died down when a Beatle spoke, to introduce the next number. During the songs, the drummer thrashed and thumped his kit so forcefully that his drum riser shook pretty much the whole time. Whenever the left-handed bassist paired with one of the other guitarists, and shared a vocal microphone, it created a mirror image; two bowl haircuts, Carnaby Street Mod suits, and guitars with their necks facing the same direction instead of in opposition. This contributed to the band's image of appealing camaraderie.

The crowd was so thrilled just to be there that, for all their over-emoting, they were remarkably orderly and well-behaved. Jelly beans were *not* lobbed onstage as projectiles, as their English fan base had taken to doing—dangerously and obsessively—after the candies were mentioned by a Beatle during a televised interview. The group performed in the standard formation, as though they were facing a typical auditorium. The setting was so inadequate to house a concert of that scale, however, that the audience was seated in the round. The band themselves felt the need to semi-rotate their equipment so that they could face a different section of the stands every few numbers.

To be on that stage—on *any* stage with that much amplification—was like being constantly bashed about and blasted with waves of vibration. It would be like being in a wind tunnel or in direct proximity to a jet engine. This would be true enough of the power of amplification in any indoor setting; but with the rudimentary acoustics of the Coliseum, essentially a massive concrete tube originally intended to house an ice skating arena, the pure sound echoed and overlapped indiscriminately. And, naturally, the ecstatic fans created a force of the own, a wall of energy cascaded over the musicians.

Back in the bus at the appointed time and place, Thomas' ears were ringing. The walls of the building still reverberated with the beat of an encore number. (You can always tell whether you're attending a concert in Washington, D.C. among power-brokers, or the humble natives. If the house is full of big-timers, they stream up the aisles towards the exits during a curtain call to be the first ones out of the parking lot.

If they're common folk, they demand multiple encores, and stay right through to the end.) At the Beatles' American premier, however, an MC ended the proceedings, thanked the ramped-up but well-behaved crowd for being so orderly, promised to deliver a fan letter for someone and predicted that the boys would be back soon.

Afterwards, the same affable foursome reentered the bus. They were bundled up in their trench coats, but as they settled back into the bus, they started removing the coats and reaching into the fridge for bottles of Dr. Pepper. Where, during the trip in, the musicians were fighting pre-performance nerves, and had been relatively subdued, at this point they were positively raucous in the aftermath of the live rock and roll rush. In any case, they were roughhousing in the back, chattering and clinking their soda bottle necks. Involuntarily, Thomas thought of how he liked to keep the dining and storage area tidy. How could four young men create such an ungodly racket? Really, what it came down to was he was unused to having company.

Thomas' instructions for after the concert involved delivering his to the British Embassy for an after party. As he merged into traffic, rounding Union Station, one of them was trying to attract his attention, but there was no way to comply at that moment. They were on Massachusetts Avenue, heading west. Though he was still unsure which Beatle was which, Thomas saw, peripherally, that it was the angular-faced darker complexioned lead guitarist who was in a crouch behind the drivers' seat. The bus had to nose into the flow of traffic—an especially delicate maneuver under bad road conditions—and Thomas had to tap the brakes. The bus lurched. This was enough to cause the Beatle's head to thump forcefully against the rear of the backrest. At that point, he'd apparently given up on trying to get anyone's attention. Thomas thought he heard a groan.

'Oh... *fudge*,' Thomas' heart fell into his stomach. 'Stick a fork in me, I'm done!' or whatever you say when you've just committed a deal-breaking blunder. For a moment, even in the act of driving, his mind was a blank except for self-pity. Then, to his intense relief, the 'victim' in the back had snapped out of it, and was on a laughing jag. No harm, no foul!

The relatively brief trip wound down uneventfully from there, and to the extent that the group settled down, they were so pleasant and friendly that Thomas' nerves were able to quiet down. He pulled up to the gate at the embassy, and the unconventional vehicle was met by a guard. The Beatles made faces at him up against the window as they were cleared for entrance.

Three members of the group bounded out of the bus, carrying their bottles with the backwash rippling. While two of them bolted for the doors, one wearing a cap paused and faced Thomas to salute him in an amused, wise-assed manner—not unlike Peter Sellers—by way of saying goodnight; the 'head wound' Beatle, who introduced himself as George, lagged behind to carry on a conversation with Thomas.

Earlier this evening, February 11th, 1964, *now*, it was all happening. The Beatles had conquered

America on the record charts, on television, and in concert.

The Beatles—and each member of every rock group in the "British Invasion" to follow—revered the rare artifacts of American culture that traveled with the sailors in dingy European ports such as the Beatle's home town of Liverpool. While post-war Britain wasn't a cultural desert, exactly, with its home parlor piano, or its club scene heavily featuring traditional Jazz or Skiffle music, none of the domestic stuff impressed novelty-starved British youth like the raw impact of Elvis, Little Richard or Jerry Lee Lewis.

It was a big deal indeed for The Beatles to become the biggest group in the North of England, and then to conquer London, but that level of fame absolutely paled in comparison to the dream come true of 'making it' in America, land of the delta blues, Memphis, and New Orleans. America was the rhythm & blues, country & western, rock 'n' roll *mecca*. And The Beatles had become the first of the English beat groups to be embraced, even adopted, by this country (once the publicity machines on both sides of the Atlantic were aligned).

George, who had become known as the 'quiet Beatle,' was on his second trip to the promised land in a little over a year. He'd visited his sister, who lived in

Illinois, in the fall of '63; his sister Louise had emigrated there with her Scottish husband. George came over with his brother Peter for a bit. It was a pleasure trip. He was comparatively anonymous, except for the fact that the Harrison family copy of the 45 of *From Me To You* had been played on local radio. He played dances backed by local bands, jammed with other musicians and shopped for guitars. This year, on the East Coast, it was different, certainly—hoards of screaming girls were stalking them everywhere they went, for one thing; it had almost gotten so a person couldn't think straight—but, if anything, the reality of America matched its allure. A young Brit, taking in the sights, couldn't help but notice how differently, and much better, the burgers and soda tasted.

Alone for a moment with Thomas, George played a little party trick he'd come up with to break the ice with in America, to use among those in general awe of rockers, or whomever else a foreigner was likely to meet so far from home. He pulled a little black book from his hip pocket, and presented it to Thomas, with a ballpoint pen. It was open to a blank page. "Here, Mate, can I have your autograph?" This always provoked a pleased reaction from the surprised American. Then George would ask them for an address, and explain that he liked to keep track of the people he'd shared something with in each of the towns on tour. It helped to make what were essentially anonymous whistle-stops seem less impersonal. Also, with the fan mail pouring in—and, along with that, the impossibility of *keeping up* with it—this small gesture gave him a measure of sanity. George called it his *Diary of American Friends.* "I'd best go, but write down your address for me, so we can stay in touch." And with that, he was gone into the night. Or, that is, he nipped into the entrance hall of the embassy.

Chapter 14 – Bangladesh

The years passed, and Thomas became something of an institution while on the job, moving up in a lateral way, within Congressional housekeeping, by quietly assuming more responsibility over time; his efforts were reflected in his gradually advanced pay grade.

Professional cleaning's a thankless task, where, when someone's performing a superior service, no one has reason to pay much attention, and Thomas made it his business to see that no one complained. His duty was keeping the offices, hallways, cafeteria and other facilities in orderly condition. In a sense, order had to be kept to counter the commotion surrounding wars and other world events and political affairs that beset Congressmen and their staffers. The wildness of the '60s transitioned into the somewhat more stable '70s, and Thomas—as an amateur scholar and historian—made note of foreign and domestic matters. He had taken to collecting discarded documents that traced the various changes.

Of course, The Beatles' career had been anything but quiet. The group broke up in 1970, after opting to quit touring years before, due to the hysteria generated by their public performances, and also to concentrate their energy in creating a series of groundbreaking studio releases. Each of the former Beatles reinvented themselves as solo artists. Collectively, each in their own way, they maintained strong ties with the United States, and the public that had treated them so well. After their meeting, Thomas became a sort of 'pen pal' with George Harrison; George was particularly loyal to his friends. This seemed to go along with his being so unimpressed with The Beatles' all-consuming fame. George would always start his letters to Thomas with "To my first American friend...," this was a tongue-in-cheek comment, just his style. Whenever Thomas received a new letter—the later ones on Apple Records stationary—he'd think, 'those cheeky Brits!'

In 1970 George was celebrating the success of his song *My Sweet Lord*, the first single by an ex-Beatle to reach #1. It went on to sell five million copies. Having a hit single as a solo artist confirmed his stature as a songwriter after years of playing a subordinate role amongst the group. During The Beatle's brief career, they were seen to represent, and speak for, world youth culture, even though they initially held out against the pressure to declare their position on the Vietnam War. But now, the South Asian state of Bangladesh, already riven by war, was suffering the effects of a devastating cyclone. Millions of people were uprooted, and suffering terribly.

George's friend, the famous Indian musician Ravi Shankar, had family ties to the affected region, and sought some way to administer aid. Shankar, speaking of his countrymen's plight, inspired the formerly quiet Beatle to use his extraordinary influence to produce a benefit concert.

The Concert for Bangladesh—held for two shows on August 1st, 1971 at Madison Square Garden—was thrown together in desperate haste but all of its elements came together so well as to defy all expectation. As overextended as George had been during the run-up to the concert, he was gentleman enough to invite Thomas. He sent tickets to the second show, in the evening, thinking that it was likely that the performers would work out the inevitable kinks by then. Short notice that it was, Thomas was excited to attend. But the VW bus needed some work; it might not be up for the rigors of a trip to New York. He would take it a neighborhood garage for repairs to be done while he was out of town.

There was a tragic bus crash on Interstate 95 between Philadelphia and New York. The concert was a total-immersion experience for George, as the headliner, and all the participants who'd come together for the event; news of the accident was never circulated within the player's entourage; in the mad rush of the days leading up to the event, it was all they could do to transcend their stage fright, all in hopes of providing some relief to the mass of Bengali victims. It's perhaps to be expected that it would never have come to George's attention that Thomas was a no-show. He never realized his old friend was killed.

The department head at the Capital Building, Thomas' supervisor, made some inquiries but had very little to go on, at least in the short term. This stuck in his craw, and he persisted in his inquiries; Thomas had never impressed him as an absentee. Ultimately, though, information about the crash fatalities trickled in independently, as distributed by the Luzerne County Coroners' Office, in Wilkes-Barre, and the Pennsylvania State Police.

After a time, Thomas' neighbor, Paul, realized that Thomas had, in fact, gone missing. As he detailed his efforts to locate information on his neighbor's whereabouts, or at least that of his bus, the boys, not for the first time, thought, "If only this bus could talk!" But the resources Paul could devote to the search were limited; his own investigation had totally fizzled out.

"I tried to find his camper," Paul told Cam and the other boys as he finished his account, "but I couldn't figure out where it was. I called every foreign car shop I could find, but was never able to locate it. I knew of no relatives other than his Aunt Marjorie, but I couldn't get through to her either. By then, she was in her mid-eighties, and I believe she was deteriorating. I read that she passed away herself a year later.

"There wasn't much of value in his room, except this photo. In a room that only measured nine by six, this picture pretty overwhelming, but he loved it. He told me that he liked to imagine what was carried on the canal, what type of vessels they used, and what type of animal was used to pull those boats. I secreted the picture away in the middle of the night before his stuff was carted away. I think my friend would have wanted me to have it.

"So, I know Thomas didn't use the second ticket that he was given to the Coliseum concert. He must have put it somewhere for safekeeping in the bus, and it sounds like you all found it. If I were you, I wouldn't sell that ticket on eBay. I think it's an important part of the history of your bus."

Chapter 15 – JFK

A major complication to the investigation of the VW bus' history—and ever really finding out the reason that it ultimately ended up on the auction block—is that Thomas (unwittingly or not,) had been engaged in an illegal activity, something perceived to be a national security risk. Once that situation came to light, and the Secret Service became involved, the story goes underground and into Official Washingtonian mythology.

Thomas had gone missing, and it had been for long enough that even people that *didn't* know him had started to wonder what was up. The back lot of the garage where he'd taken the bus for repairs was funky, oil slick and grime encrusted, and housed a number of picked-over auto chassis and junkers that had been salvaged for parts and left for dead. As viable cars came in, received maintenance, and left, the parked VW bus was starting to look increasingly abandoned and out of place.

It had been forty-five days, and it had reached the point that the garage—as Thomas Michael Post's creditor, based on the unpaid repairs and storage fees—assumed a lien on the vehicle. What management needed to do at that juncture was to apply for a certificate to put the bus up for auction through the District Court. There wasn't a great deal of incentive the garage to do so; most businesses left in the lurch didn't relish having to go through the system to recoup a loss. There wasn't much money to be made by doing so. For the most part, property divested in this manner barely cleared expenses, as the bidding tended to skew pretty low, of course. Once the city clerk's office fees have been settled, it was hardly worthwhile. But it certainly beat paying out for the offending vehicle to be towed to the dump.

So, grudgingly, during some down time, a junior grease monkey was instructed to take the key from the plastic sleeve containing the VW's work order; his objective was to go through the bus' interior for some additional identification, some last-ditch resource that might connect this abandoned vehicle to its absentee owner. The garage employee went in to examine the

106

contents of the glove compartment. However, anyone familiar with a 1963, air-cooled VW bus knows that they *have* no glove compartment. But there're two oblong, vertical closets toward the rear of the kitchen interior. Popping one of the closets open, the seeker came upon Thomas' secret.

Moments later, he walked back into the rear office with a bankers' box marked "Property of United States Congress," and containing reams of mismatched documents in a patchwork system of manila envelopes and hanging file folders. Thomas' closets contained several such boxes, stacked from floor to ceiling. Each artifact contained within was no more than a few pages long, but there were many, many. Thomas hadn't been a janitor so much as a hoarder.

Each document or set of papers dealt with some random bit of the minutia of the John F. Kennedy administration. He'd made an attempt to keep his treasures in something resembling chronological order, or at least the order in which he acquired the papers when extracting them from the old circular file. While Thomas definitely dealt in quantity as opposed to quality, there must have been some sensitive material secreted in all that waste paper, but it would've taken a highly determined individual to locate some confidential or otherwise incriminating item in the stash. As ever, Thomas meant well; he was no subversive, trying to bring down the government from within. But he was breaking the law, at a federal level.

In point of fact, his practice of keeping the occasional official document—policy proposals, directives, interoffice memos—as a sort of keepsake of the Kennedy Administration—had already begun shortly after Thomas assumed his duties. He saw it as preserving the Kennedy legacy for posterity. In a sense, he had a point. The John F. Kennedy Presidential Library, in Boston, wouldn't be dedicated until 1977. While the National Archives and Records Administration looked after J.F.K's significant papers, Thomas appointed himself to keep track of the paperwork that was considered disposable in the short term, but might turn out to be significant in the future. As to his right to the material he fished out of the trash, in official terms, he was like the guy in the

Johnny Cash song who, while working on the GM assembly line, steals a Cadillac by taking home a part at a time in his lunch box.

Then came the horrible day in November. The 22nd, 1963; the assassination. His hero gone, Thomas coped, along with the country, as best as he could. Later, when he discovered that paperwork from the Johnson Administration didn't have that same glamor, that Kennedy *joie de vivre*, he transferred his attentions to Robert Kennedy, collecting documents from the Secretary of State's office whenever the opportunity presented itself.

Once the contents of the boxes in the bus were determined, the disposal of the vehicle was no longer the province of the city clerk. The Secret Service cordoned off the back lot of the garage, in a sort of belated damage-control maneuver. All of Thomas' idols (he had some residual respect, but no special feeling, for Ted Kennedy) had predeceased him. In the eyes of the authorities, though, suspicious activities, signifying a potentially dangerous stalker, kook, or foreign agent, had come to light. The vehicle was confiscated, along with its contents, for processing.

This was the background of the Federal suit, "The United States of American vs. one 1963 Volkswagen Camper." The impounded camper moved through channels until it was quietly auctioned off through Weschler's Auction House, with the legally required notices in hyper-small print in The Washington Post and the Washington Law Review. After the auction, when it left the government's care, it was never officially seen again.

Some documentation on file, regarding the original city repossession, in the District Court's warehouses ended up being lost or destroyed long before Cameron and the boys could have ever found it and used it to reconstruct a paper trail for the bus. Actually, the Secret Service—as a sort of legal cover-up maneuver—made it their practice to file *anything* they didn't want to be known with the District Court, fully expecting it to disappear as though it had never even existed.

So, even though the secret of the court case has been buried forever, the situation involving the Beatle's concert ticket was ongoing. The hidden world of the bus encompassed both a political cover up, and, subsequently, Howard Morders' personal intrigue.

Chapter 16 – Snipe

The boys sat for a couple minutes, dumbfounded. Cameron started to think of how he hadn't told his dad about the ticket, which had now backfired on him. The item that was key to the history of the bus... was about to be sold online.

The boys looked at each other. They all knew, somehow they needed to make sure that the ticket did not get sold.

Cameron sat at the dinner table, virtually unable to swallow a thing. He needed to tell his dad, but kept putting it off. The problem was the clock... The eBay clock, that is. It was ticking away the time. Even now, acquisitive rock memorabilia freaks were automatically updating their bids in increments of a dollar over those of their competitors, a practice known as "sniping."

"Dad, I need to discuss something with you. I've made a horrible mistake." Well, now that he had started, it was all going to come rolling off his tongue, like it or not.

"I found a small treasure in your Volkswagen bus. Um, actually I didn't know it was a treasure, for sure, when I found it. But now I know it is, and I've already had Jay's dad put it for sale on eBay. Now it's gonna be sold, and Dad, we can't let it be sold."

The first thought that entered his dad's mind was "Have they started experimenting with beer at twelve? He's babbling." But a close look at Cameron's face revealed the seriousness, and sobriety, of the message.

"O.K., so you found a treasure. In the bus?" "Yes."

"Jewelry? Money?" "No. It's a concert ticket from the '60s."

"Ohhh-kay," his dad was quickly losing interest. This was starting to sound like a little game. Sort of like 'seventh grade humor.' He had better things to do. Like eat dinner, and get with the evening's relaxation.

Hopefully this wasn't going to be a 'help with the homework' night.

"No dad. It's valuable. Jay's dad put it on eBay, and it's been bid to over one thousand dollars. Actually, thirteen hundred and forty dollars. We three guys were going to split it, for some summer pocket money. Sorry dad, I should have told you."

"Wow. Well, you kinda screwed up by not telling me. Now, I guess it'll be my windfall. And maybe you guys will have earned a portion as a finder's fee. That'll teach you a lesson, because if you'd informed me of the find, I probably would have let you keep it all."

"Thanks for being understanding Dad; but, there's a problem. We've been doing some research on the history of your bus."

"Actually Cameron, that's admirable. Sounds like it's been a good summer project for you guys. Smart."

"Well, dad, it's what we found out. See, the ticket is an unused ticket from the very, very first concert of The Beatles in the United States. It's from February of 1964." His dad was impressed. "Cameron, that's cool."

"Problem is, in our search, we found out the original owner of the bus—the original owner, the guy named Thomas Post—we found out he was hired to chauffeur The Beatles to the concert. In your bus. Dad, it's not only valuable, it's really an artifact associated with your bus. I think it's a piece of rock and roll history, and it belongs with your bus, and now we've stupidly put it on eBay."

Cameron started crying. Once he started, being a sensitive kid, there was no stopping. Through his tears, he blurted out, "I don't think we can stop it from selling."

His dad had to process all this; it was a lot. His bus. His bus had taken The Beatles to their first concert. Had he heard it right? Wait, this made no sense. Where was their first concert? In the United Kingdom. Or, if in America, certainly in New York.

And now he was getting stressed confused. (Yes, those two words do go together sometimes.) He was straight-up confused. His look through the history of the bus had indicated that it was a Washington, D.C.-based bus, going back to almost new. He had, in the papers, a registration from the '60s or early '70s; a D.C. registration.

"The Beatles? Cam, my bus has been in D.C. almost its entire life. We know the original owner drove it from California, stopped at National Parks and got all those decals. But I think he got to Washington very early. That wouldn't match with a history of The Beatles..."

"Dad, we did research it. We went out and met people. And we learned the first concert by The Beatles was actually at the old Coliseum, near Union Station."

"You're kidding. Are you sure it really has a Beatles history? That's pretty neat." His dad was silent for a while and then said, "I'll call Jay's dad and we'll figure it out."

After the meal, his dad retreated to his study. He closed the door but didn't fully shut it. The message was, 'this was going to be a private call.'

Cameron stood within earshot, but he couldn't really make it out. His dad's voice sounded excited, then serious. It went on for quite a while. Finally he came out.

"Cameron. You put something up for sale, and you can't welch on it. Your honor is at stake. And your friends'. When you commit to something, you have to see it through. Plus, Jay's dad used his membership on eBay. He's not going to put that at risk. In today's world, your reputation online is very important. It's really neat that the bus might have been used to carry The Beatles. But, the ticket and the bus will just have to go separate ways. We'll see what to do with the money once the auction ends."

The next day it did end. More bidders came in. There was a bidding frenzy in the last five minutes. And faster than any human could possibly tap in bids, the numbers soared in the last five seconds. Bidders were using automated services to tender their high bids. It ultimately landed at five thousand, one hundred and twelve dollars. Evidently, the second high bidder had placed a proxy bid at $5111.00. He'd used one of many bidding services, and figured that he was comfortable at about five thousand. But, if necessary, he was going to be one hundred more than the next guy at five thousand, or ten more, or one more. The only problem was that one more bidder was higher than him, and so all it took was for the system to bid a buck higher than the number two bidder.

They carefully enveloped, wrapped, bagged, boxed and insured the sold ticket. It was FedExed to the buyer, at his expense, in California. The 'buyer' was a gallery, most likely a dealer buying for stock. When the new owner found a collector who just had to have the only unused ticket of its kind in existence, it was going to change hands at a much higher price. Someday it would probably end up in a museum or an institutional collection, and be on display in a frame many times its size. But for now, it was going to be inventory.

Chapter 17 – Serpentine

The name "Post," as in Thomas Michael, is so ubiquitous as to be impossible to trace on a search engine. The boy detectives had come to a dead end. On the other hand, *Morders* was a name that the boys could work with; Morders, of course, being the name of the person that acquired the van formerly owned by Thomas. While the commercial enterprise, Howard Morders' garage, left no internet footprint behind—there being no specific photo record or documentation available—Morders' family history came up in form of a census listing on Ancestry.com. A search of the 1930s U.S. Census documentation alluded to a family, based in Bethesda, Maryland, and a son, just starting out in his trade. Howard Morders was listed as an "Auto Trimmer."

The main thing was there was a trail, and beyond that, someone within the extended family had taken it upon themselves to create a family tree. Although, as it turned out, most of the members of the tree were either deceased or listed anonymously, the boys found Howard's one surviving relative, although she was listed by name only. They would have to keep digging for supporting information. Cam contacted the administrator of that tree, with an appeal that included some of the details of their search. He was sure to include his—and the others'—ages. The boys had figured out that they likely to be granted access and entrée to certain places or information because some adults regarded them as "adorable," playing at being all grown-up. It was assumed that their parents must know what they were up to and that they must be working on some elaborate school project, and who wouldn't want to cooperate with such earnest junior detectives? Long story short, the family tree admin forwarded their request to contact the surviving Morder, who as it turns out, was Howard's sister.

She emailed that her address was in Charlottesville, and it would be no problem for her to fill them in on her brother and tell them what she knew about the bus. The conversation itself could've been done over the phone. She didn't want to necessarily impose a trip to Charlottesville on the boys, strangers at that, purely on the basis of her family's, and Cam's, ownership of the bus. But, she said there was also a compelling reason that they might want to actually come visit her; something about "closure." But it was a surprise and she didn't want to spoil it for them, as it was bound up in the story.

The former Ms. Morders, now Mrs. Jack, was a faculty wife at the University of Virginia. This news was welcomed, in terms of the overall investigation. That didn't seem like too much of a faraway locale; especially since each of the three boys had at least one parent who'd graduated from the University. Cameron's Mom, Zach's Mom, and both Jay's parents were alumni. So the boys had a passing familiarity with the campus, and Jay knew facts and trivia of its history. Besides the university connection to Thomas Jefferson—which was official stuff they were taught in class—it was the school that Edgar Allen Poe attended, there to spend his formative years practicing journalism.

The boys were curious, and spent very little time wondering if the trip was justified. It was a direct trip, and only about two hours each way. They reasoned that they could do it all in one afternoon and never be missed, so they hopped on the Northeast Regional at the Alexandria Station.

The University of Virginia is ultra-convenient to get to by train. The tracks pass right through campus, and the adjacent commercial district, or The Corner, the site for a concentration of restaurants, bars, and other student body amenities.

Although the tracks ran close to their destination, the station was a hike down Main Street. They stepped off the train from Washington and were face to face with a Wild Wing Café. Evidently the larger train station building was no longer necessary for its original use, and so it had been leased out for a restaurant.

"I'm game for some wings," said Jay. "Jay, that's why we brought bag lunches, so we could stick to business and make sure we get back home on time. I for one do not want to get nailed because of this journey." "Me neither!" joined in Zach. "O.K., but if we have time on the way back, I do want some ribs," added Jay. And they started marching down the sidewalk towards the campus.

"Cupcakes!" said Jay as he spied a bakery. "Jay... Keep movin," said Cameron. Once they arrived in the section known as The Corner, Jay knew the way to get to The Lawn. Once again Jay was tempted, this time by the scent of fresh bagels, but he pressed on.

The boy detectives passed Mincer's UVA Imprinted Sportswear, and ultimately found themselves on The Lawn, the onetime most ambitious architectural installation in the country, along with Jefferson's Monticello.

They approached Professor Carson Jack's pavilion home on the campus grounds. The Rotunda presided over the pavilion residences and the student rooms known as Lawn rooms, and other buildings in Jefferson's "Academical Village." Each pavilion had its own walled-in garden. The walls themselves were a notable feature, even if their twisting and turning was somewhat odd-looking to Zach. "What's with the snaky walls?" he said. Jay was ready with an answer; truth to tell, there were a lot of questions Jay was prepared to answer that never even got asked. "That's a style called 'serpentine.' It was designed by Thomas Jefferson."

Cam, a bit disoriented, and looking at the slip of paper with Mrs. Jack's directions, was glad to have a momentary diversion. "You think these have been around that long?" Jay answered, "Yeah, actually, that's the thing. The design is based on the idea that if you build the brickwork in curved patterns, it's stronger. It's the thinnest, but most durable wall you can make."

Zach was thinking, 'that's more than enough to know about brick walls,' but asked, "So where's the house?" Cam told them that Mrs. Jack said the place they were looking for was "on The Lawn." Zach made an expression and gesture like, 'So? We're *all* on the lawn."

Jay was having a factoid field day. "The Lawn is a central area of grass, and the famous Rotunda is there," he pointed, although the point he was making was fairly obvious, considering the highly distinctive shape of that building. "Also designed by Mr. Jefferson." Cam, not to be outdone, offered, "You know, they call this place 'The University.' And when you say that on the East Coast, everybody's supposed to know that you're talking about Virginia." "Sounds kinda uppity to me," Jay said, half kidding. "Well, universities are quite competitive," Cam said, in conclusion.

"O.K., so this is clearly The Lawn." Jay said. "We're looking for the Birdwood Carriage house." Zach peered around, "So they live in one of these nice houses. Who gets the teeny rooms?" Cam explained a finer point of university life. "Actually the rooms between the nice homes are very prestigious to live in. You have to be an upper classman or something. It's weird, they don't have bathrooms, but you do get a nice fireplace." "Oh, that's important," Zach wise-assed. Cam said, "Well, in the winter it might be," because, when you thought about it, that was probably true.

The boys walked along the sidewalk and were heading in the direction of the Rotunda. "It burned, you know..." Jay said, referring to the main building. Cam thought he'd heard something to that effect. "The Rotunda?" "Yup. It was a long time ago. But I've seen photos of people standing right out here, watching the fire." The mention of destruction made Zach's interest perk up. "Have you ever been in it?" "Yup, it's neat," Jay said.

They were coming up to a small, but elegant, white columned house. Cam-announced, "O.K., here's the place." They knocked. After a few moments, an older man answered. He looked like a professor; he dressed the part, too, in a tweed jacket and cords. Professor Jack motioned for them to enter. "Hello boys. I guess my wife has been expecting you. She will be happy to see that you made it here. By the way, did you tell your parents you were coming down here?"

"Yes sir," said Cameron. "We did."

"Well, I'm Doctor Jack. Come on in."

They entered a room that looked like a room in a museum. A museum of the 1800s. It featured brass lamps, oil paintings, slender-armed wooden chairs, and upholstered couches. He led them through a couple of rooms until he indicated for them to sit down. The Professor said, "Make yourselves comfy. I'll get my missus," and left.

After a couple of minutes, she entered the room without her husband. She kind of looked like the wicked witch from the Wizard of Oz, Cam thought, with a beaky nose and spindly features. But, Cam also thought, more charitably, she might have been nice-looking when she was younger, when her brother was alive. Back in the day, she might have had fine features, with what they call an 'aquiline' nose. But now, she was wearing a dress like no self-respecting younger woman would wear, a farmer's wife dress. She held her hand out for the boys to shake, in turn. Her hand was thin and heavily veined, and felt papery in theirs.

"I'm Cameron, Mrs. Morders... I mean *Jack*. Sorry." Mrs. Jack said, "I'm pleased to meet you, Mr.

Luther. It sounds good to have someone call me Mrs. Morders. That takes me back to a distant past. My husband and I have been married for fifty-two years."

"Yes, ma'am. It's nice to meet *you*."

"I'm Jay." "Hello. And you must be Zach." (They had gone over all their personal information previously, over the phone.) She motioned for them to sit down, along with her. Cam said, "You have a lovely home here, ma'am." She smiled.

Mrs. Jack decided to get to the point. "So how's the bus?" Cam was a little surprised that she initiated the topic, even if they'd spoken of it earlier. "Did you know the bus, ma'am?" "Well, actually I never saw it. I just knew about it. My brother told me that it was very special to him."

"Really? Cam asked, "Why?" *Now* they were in uncharted territory.

"Well, where do we start?" she mused. "Do you boys know what my brother Howard did for a living?" "Yes ma'am. We know he had an upholstery business.

Auto upholstery." Jay specified. "That's right," she said. "He started as an automobile trimmer as a very young man, and did it all his life. But that was his vocation, not his love."

"His love, ma'am?" asked Cam. The boys glanced at each other; things had suddenly gotten sort of deep.

Mrs. Jack continued, aware of the boy's surprise, but figuring they'd be able to follow the mature path the conversation had taken. "His love was music. And you know, he never married. So he led kind of a lonely life. He did his work, and after work he would enjoy his music. I had six other siblings, but Howard and I were closest over the years. We didn't spend much time together, but we stayed in touch by letter and phone."

Howard bought many records and loved to listen to them. He would also occasionally concerts.

He considered himself fortunate to acquire one of those concert tickets in 1964, to see the Beatles. After that, they were always his favorite performers. He told me that particular concert was their first in the United States, and he'd seen them perform on the Ed Sullivan Show two nights before that. He had been able to get a ticket, but the weather was terrible. There was snow on the ground and he ended up walking for part of the way to reach the auditorium. Afterwards, he'd always thought of it as having been well worth the effort.

Being in the automobile business, he often had an opportunity to get a good deal on a car. Particularly in Washington, D.C., a town with a transient work force, with administrations that turn over every four years, someone's always leaving in a hurry. They may be a diplomat called back home to their country, or someone with the government post being quickly abruptly stationed overseas. And they'd want to sell their car in a hurry.

In one instance, he'd learned that another automobile business, a neighbor of his shop, was to auction a vehicle. And it was a Volkswagen bus.

Howard went to take a look at it, and he could not believe his eyes.

He knew *this* bus. He'd seen it about eight years before this auction, when he walked through the snow to attend the concert. Well, at first he wasn't sure, but he knew it was the same color. A dark green and white.

So he looked closely at the bus. Because when he'd seen the same colored bus at the concert, he remembered those specific decals in the windows, the decals for Yellowstone National Park and Yosemite.

And sure enough, this bus at the auction had those decals. Howard had seen the rock band embark from the bus in the snowy parking lot of the auditorium. He just happened to be standing nearby, admiring the bus, and he said they came piling out. He was close enough to recognize the boys.

He told no one of the history of the bus to be auctioned. At the designated time, a couple days later, he came back for the auction. The bus was his for a couple hundred dollars.

He immediately took it back to the warehouse his business was in. And that same day, it was loaded into the freight elevator and taken to the third floor. That bus sat in that spot for the remainder of his life, about twenty years.

Cam, Zach and Jay had been hanging on to every word of the amazing story. But it made no sense to them that if someone owned such a cool vehicle, that he wouldn't make extensive use of it. When you thought about it, the adult world could be pretty perplexing.

"Why didn't he drive it?" asked Cam.

"Why didn't he drive it??" countered Mrs. Jack, as though the answer were self-evident. "He *worshipped* it. He said that it was the vehicle which delivered the Beatles to their very first concert in the United States. He said it was a seminal moment in the history of music. Of culture. He said the bus was a National Treasure. He told me—and of course I knew this was just a lonely guy's opinion—he told me that it belonged in the Smithsonian Institution. But he kept it for himself. It was his treasure. It was his way to get close to his idols.

Zach asked, "Just wonderin' ma'am...but *how* did he worship it? I mean, it's not like he prayed to it, right? He didn't use it as an altar, did he?"

"No, of course not," said Mrs. Jack indulgently, now laughing. "Remember, my brother loved their music..."

She was sitting across from the boys, but now she leaned her body forward and jutted her head towards them. She glanced around, as if to make sure no one was watching or listening. It was unlikely that there would be anyone listening, unless maybe her husband was in the next room with his ear to the wall. She was getting ready to tell them something, and from her body language it was clear that this was for them only. This was like a special secret.

"Howard would listen to music in the bus. Their music. Only their music. He had an old portable record player, a wind-up model, and his stash of

Beatles records. When he closed up the shop for the day, he would pour himself a little glass of red wine. And he would go up to the third floor and climb in the bus. He told me that he'd never been happier in his life then he was during those times. He'd wind up the record player and listen to a Beatles album. And he never tired of those songs.

"He'd spend about a half an hour in the bus, and then he'd go home. But in that bus, he was not alone. No way. He said it was still inhabited with a little of the spirit of George, John, Paul, and Ringo. It was just him and them, and their music. That was his little bit of Heaven.

"So boys, that ended about twenty years ago when my brother passed away. I was very pleased to hear from you all, it brought back the good memories of my brother. It may sound like he led a lonely life, and he did... But, also, he was happy."

A moment passed after Mrs. Jack's revelation. The room was quiet. "Cameron, I want you to get something for me," she said.

He assented. She pointed towards a door in the corner. Walk over to that door. It's a closet. Please open the door. Cameron did as she asked. "Now, down on the floor, behind the coats are two small suitcases. Please bring them here."

Cameron pushed away the coats and reached in to feel for handles. And then he lifted them and brought them out in the room.

"When Howard died, I didn't go into Washington to his place of business. There was really no reason for me to go there. But I did tell them I wanted one thing. I asked one of his employees to go to the third floor. I told him that there would be a record player and records in the bus, and I wanted them sent to me in Charlottesville. And they've been in that closet ever since. Cameron, I think Howard would want you to have them. And they should be with the bus. If Howard was right, and it is a treasure, then the player and records and the bus belong together. It sounds like you will be a good steward of all that.

The boys unlatched the player and marveled at its condition. The finish was maroon, which was probably plastic, but was beautifully polished, like a brand new, unused bowling ball. The brand was RCA Victor, which was spelled out in small golden letters. The other case must have had eight Beatles albums. The boys carefully read the backs of each case to see which songs were included.

After a little more chatting, they needed to get back to the train station. If they missed the train, they were going to get in big trouble with their parents.

So they walked to the station, carrying their treasures, stopping only to share a mint chocolate chip cupcake at SweetHaus. It wasn't much to split three ways, but there was a mountain of frosting to go around.

****

Who might they tell about what they'd learned? And how should they announce the news? Was this something they could put on Twitter and people from all over would want to hear the story?

The boys agreed that they would make a decision together before they did anything. And first, upon arriving back in town, they had some business to attend to....

The boys converged upon the garage, player and albums in hand. They filed in and found each of their favorite spots inside the bus. The player was set upon the 'kitchen table' and the first album was readied.

What a glorious sound. In a way, the inside of the bus felt like a chapel.

There were spirits in the van. Howard Morders was present, all alone, holding his tiny glass of wine and enjoying the music. Thomas Michael Post was up front, behind the wheel, on his way to the Capitol. In the front passenger seat was Marjorie Merriweather Post, holding on tight to the grab handle as they rushed through Rock Creek, and without a care in the world. In back were the boys. Happily listening to music were Cameron, Jay and Zach. But they weren't the only boys in the back. There was also George, John, Paul, and Ringo. Drinking their Dr. Peppers.

The three young boys made a decision. This was going to be a better decision than their eBay undertaking. They decided it would be best to keep the bus a temple they would know about, and enjoy themselves. The secrets would be safe with them.

www.ingramcontent.com/pod-product-compliance
Lightning Source LLC
Chambersburg PA
CBHW071305130626
46556CB00003B/1472